BABY BIZ is Outside

WRITTEN BY

DEBRICKA S. TAYLOR

ILLUSTRATED BY

RENIKE

ISBN: 978-0-578-95587-2

Printed in the United States of America.

First Printing 2021.

This book is dedicated to my brother
ItsBizkit (The Biggest Blogger in the World)
for his inspiration, my mother for believing in
me, and my sister, Elise for her vision.

It's morning time. Mom says,"No more sleep, it is time to rise. The sun is awake with open eyes."

Baby Biz sits up in bed. He rubs his eyes with a bright smile on his face. He feels so ready for the new day.

He darts to the bathroom to brush his teeth. Back and forth, round and round. *SWISHA, SWISHA, SWISH*.

He zooms downstairs to the kitchen to eat. Chewing and munching his cereal. *YUMMY, YUM, YUM*.

Mom says, "*HURRY, BABY BIZ. QUICK GET YOUR SHOES!*"

He says, "*I KNOW WHICH PAIR I WILL CHOOSE.*"

Look, he's outside at his favorite place, the park! He runs so fast that he feels like he can fly. He holds out his arms like a bird.

Baby Biz says, "*WATCH ME SPREAD MY WINGS AND GO UP HIGH.*"

Baby Biz says, "Look at me swing with my feet to the sky. Look at me slide with my arms open wide."

Baby Biz sees his friends have arrived at the park.

"YERRRRRRRR!!" he calls out.

They are all excited to dance, play, and sing!

Look at them play. This is a great day.

Look at them laugh, from joking around.

Now listen to Baby Biz rap. He's made a really good song.

Come on, it's your turn to sing along.

"We outside with it!"

"We outside with it!"

"You know the vibes with it!"

"We outside with it!"

Hear them rap, the girls and boys, they're filled up with lots of joy.

Now it is dark. Baby Biz and his friends must leave the park.

Mom says, "We are home, Baby Biz, it is time for bed. The moon is awake, so close your eyes."

Tomorrow will be a new day for Baby Biz to be outside.